# *The* FROG HOUSE

### MARK TAYLOR

*Illustrated by*

# BARBARA GARRISON

DUTTON CHILDREN'S BOOKS ❧ NEW YORK

CIP Data is available.

Published in the United States by
*Dutton Children's Books,*
a division of Penguin Young Readers Group
345 Hudson Street, New York, New York 10014
www.penguin.com

Designed by Heather Wood
Manufactured in China / First Edition
1   3   5   7   9   10   8   6   4   2
ISBN 0-525-46174-4

## NOTES ON THE ART

The art for this book is a series of collagraphs, a word that comes from *collage* and *graphic*. The artist begins with a heavy piece of smooth cardboard. Pieces of paper of different textures, fabric, string, and even feathers are glued in layers onto the cardboard "plate" to form the image. Some smooth areas of the cardboard may be cut and peeled away. Many of the collagraph plates in this book include dried leaves from apple trees. Gesso is painted over the entire plate, adding additional texture and definition. Several coats of acrylic medium are then applied and allowed to dry thoroughly.

Next, the artist prints her collagraphs "intaglio." Ink is spread over the entire plate, then the surface ink is wiped off. The plate is then placed faceup on an etching press and covered with a damp piece of 100 percent rag paper. Felt blankets are placed on top, and then the plate is passed through the press.

Finally, watercolor washes are added to each individual print.

*For*

GARRETT & ANNA

*and in memory of*

GLENN DUDDLES,

*a family friend who built the frog house*

M.T.

*For*

LARRY

B.G.

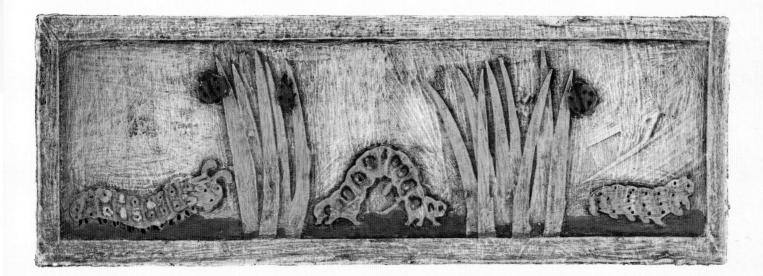

$O$ne day,
a father and his son and daughter
put a birdhouse in a tree. The
birdhouse was very special. It had
been made to look just like a big,
ripe red apple.

A little green tree frog watched
them from a branch in the tree.

The frog was curious about why they were putting an apple into a tree. He knew that people took apples *out* of trees. So the frog decided to take a closer look. When he climbed down, he was surprised to see a round hole in the apple.

The frog poked his head into the hole. He was amazed.
The apple was made of wood! And it was empty. So he
hopped inside.

The frog had seen birds move into birdhouses but never into a wooden apple. The people must have put this apple here just for me, he thought. It must be a frog house.

So he decided to move in. The frog gathered his things
and set out to make the apple a nice place to live.

Just as he had everything settled, he heard a loud knocking on his house. The frog looked out the hole to see a bird pecking at the apple. The frog yelled to the bird, "Hey! Stop that! You're going to hurt my house."

The bird was very surprised to see a frog come out of the apple. "I'm very sorry. I didn't know this was your house. I thought it was a real apple. I was going to look for worms in it. I'm a robin, and robins eat worms."

"Why don't you go look for worms in the ground?" suggested the tree frog. Then he hopped back into his house.

The frog arranged his furniture, and then he felt tired.
So he decided to take a nap. As the frog lay down and
closed his eyes, his apple house began to rock alarmingly
from side to side.

The frog was very frightened, but he managed to call out, "Stop that!" The rocking stopped, and the frog poked his head out of the hole.

A big black crow was pushing the house back and forth with his long beak. He was very surprised to see a frog in the apple. "Oh, me! I am very sorry, frog. I didn't mean to scare you. I was going to take this apple to my nest."

"I'm a crow, and crows like bright things. But I see now it is your home. So I won't take it."

The tree frog gave the crow some colorful ribbon instead. "Oh, this will do just fine," the crow said, and flew away.

After the crow was gone, the frog began to relax and wonder who would show up next. Before the frog had moved into the house, he had never had so much company.

Soon the tree frog heard a fluttering of wings and pretty chirping from outside his house. The frog looked out and saw a beautiful bluebird perched near his apple. The bluebird asked, "What are you doing in a birdhouse?"

"A birdhouse?" cried the frog. "Why, this is a *frog house*. Have you ever seen a birdhouse that looks like an apple?"

"Well," answered the bird, "now that you mention it— no. I was thinking of moving in. I'm a bird, and birds live in birdhouses. But a bird can't live in a frog house, now can it?" So the bluebird flew off.

Before the frog could even pull his head back out of the hole, he saw a big gray squirrel dashing up the tree trunk toward his house.

When the squirrel reached the apple, the frog hopped out. "What are you so excited about?" he asked.

"I'm excited because I found this juicy red apple for
lunch, and I'm going to take a big bite out of it," answered
the squirrel.

Before the tree frog could explain that the apple was made of wood, the squirrel had opened his mouth to take a bite. He yelled out in surprise, "Ow! My tooth! This is the hardest apple I've ever bitten into."

"This is not a real apple," said the frog. "It's a frog
house for a tree frog."

"Well, whatever it is, it tastes terrible. I will leave you the
apple for your house and go look for a real apple or some
nuts. I'm a squirrel, and squirrels eat nuts and fruits." And
with that, he ran down the tree.

The frog hopped back into his house to resume his nap. But he had a feeling he was being watched. The frog got up and poked his head out of his house. A furry orange cat was perched on a branch not far from the apple, staring at him.

The tree frog had never been so close to a cat before and felt uneasy. The cat meowed in an unpleasant manner. "You are the strangest-looking bird I ever saw," said the cat.

"A bird? A bird?! Do I look like a bird to you?" said the tree frog nervously. "See my long legs and green skin? I'm a tree frog."

The cat looked disappointed. "Oh, yes, I see now that you are a frog. But what are you doing in a birdhouse? I was so hoping for a bird. I'm a cat, and cats eat birds."

The frog said, "This is not a birdhouse, it's a frog house. Have you ever seen a birdhouse that looked like an apple?"

"No, I haven't," said the cat.

"Of course not," said the frog. "That's because frog houses look like apples. Now run along, but don't bother any birds. All the ones I've met seem like nice friends." The cat climbed down the tree to try his luck with mice.

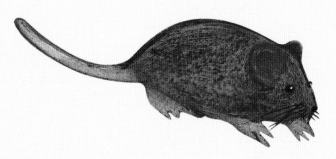

The frog didn't feel tired anymore. Now he wanted
to stay awake and see who else would come calling at his
beautiful frog house. But there were no more hungry visitors.
    And he missed them! He would sit at the hole, all by
himself, singing spring peeping songs. He was quite proud
of his voice, just as he was quite proud of his house.

One day, a beautiful green tree frog heard his song
and hopped up beside him. "What a magnificent house
you have," she said. "I don't believe I've ever seen
anything like it."

"Do come in and look around," the tree frog said to her.
And she did. She admired *everything*. . . .

And she stayed.